Me, Dad, & Number 6

DANA ANDREW JENNINGS

Illustrated by GORO SASAKI

GULLIVER BOOKS

HARCOURT BRACE & COMPANY

San Diego   New York   London

Special thanks to Michael Jennings,
Rich and Dee Hayes, and Tom Neff   —D. A. J.

Requests for permission to make copies of any part of the work should be
mailed to: Permissions Department, Harcourt Brace & Company,
6277 Sea Harbor Drive, Orlando, Florida 32887-6777.

Library of Congress Cataloging-in-Publication Data
Jennings, Dana Andrew.
Me, Dad, & Number 6/Dana Andrew Jennings;
illustrated by Goro Sasaki.—1st ed.
p.   cm.
"Gulliver Books."
Summary: A father, his friends, and his six-year-old son
rebuild an old car together and drive it in races.
ISBN 0-15-200085-2
[1. Fathers and sons—Fiction. 2. Automobiles—Fiction.
3. Stock car racing—Fiction.] I. Sasaki, Goro, ill. II. Title.
III. Title: Me, Dad, & Number 6.
PZ7.J42982Me   1997
[E]—dc20   93–43640
First edition
A C E F D B

Printed in Singapore

The illustrations in this book were done in Winsor & Newton
watercolor paint on Arches cold-press watercolor paper.
The display type was set in Craw Modern.
The text type was set in Fairfield Medium.
Color separations by Rainbow Graphic Arts, Ltd., Hong Kong
Printed and bound by Tien Wah Press, Singapore
This book was printed on Nymolla Matte Art paper.
Production supervision by Stan Redfern
Designed by Kaelin Chappell

To Drew —D. A. J.

To my wife, Emi, and my daughter, Mayu —G. S.

My dad works real hard at Cheney's Mill. Some nights he doesn't come home till late, and his good-night kisses smell like sawdust. Most Saturdays he sleeps till noon—if Mom lets him.

But one Saturday in March, Dad got up with the moon still in the sky. He disappeared for the morning, and the house drowsed quiet without his grizzly bear snores. Then I played—winging my red rubber ball at the barn door, counting and recounting my bottle caps, racing my shadow—and I tried to figure out what'd got Dad up and out of his warm weekend bed. The only other time I'd seen him rise before ten on a Saturday was once when Mom doused him with a bucket brimming with ice-cold well water. I suppose she was mad at him about something.

When Dad's pickup—Dad and his buddies, Dick and Orrie, jammed in the front—finally jounced back into the dooryard, the truck had an old black car in tow. Scrawled in the car's windshield dust was: 4 SALE—$20.

"Where'd you get the car, Daddy?" I asked, slopping across the muddy dooryard. "What're you going to do with it?"

"Just you wait and see." Dad grinned. "Just you wait."

Dad and Dick and Orrie worked over that car, a 1937 Pontiac coupe, in our barn for two months solid. Before work...after work...Saturdays...Sundays. And I helped.

I handed them wrenches and pliers and screwdrivers. I sanded rust off the chrome. I fetched Cokes from the house. I hunted for lost washers, nuts, and screws. And best of all, I got as garage grungy as I possibly could.

After working on the car, Dad and I'd trudge toward the house all greasy and grimy, looking like grubby monsters that lived in a tailpipe. Mom took it pretty good. She'd shake her head, half smile, and toss us Dad's gritty sandsoap that always leaves your skin red and sting-y.

The first Sunday in May, Dad woke me and carried me outside just as the morning sun poked over the trees. He'd been up all night, and his barbwire whiskers scratched my cheek.

"Watch this," he whispered—I could see his breath—and then he shouted, "Crank it, Orrie!"

The Pontiac bellowed to life in the barn, then rumbled into the dooryard, where it idled and grumbled. That car was as black and shiny as a raven's wing, and fresh-splashed on its door in bright red paint was the number 6—my age.

"It's beautiful, Daddy," I said. "Just beautiful. Are we going to race it?"

"Yup." Dad nodded. "We're going to go racing. There's more to living than working at that old sawmill."

I loved going to the races. Loved how the roar of the stock cars prickled my ears and shimmied in my belly. Loved how the cars spit fire and *whoosh*ed wind as they jabbed, jostled, and jammed around the track. Loved the smell of burnt rubber, grease, gasoline, and hot steel.

Dad drove Number 6, and sometimes after the races he'd take me out on the track. He'd let me wear the helmet and the bandanna for my mouth and nose, and help me guide the steering wheel as we did lazy turns around the oval.

"I could stay out here forever, Andy," he'd say.

"Me, too," I'd say.

Number 6 never won a race. But Dad goosed her into third place a few times and even second once. I kept the trophies in my room and dusted them at least twice a week; the little bit of money we won went back into the car.

The last Sunday of that racing season, there were more than forty cars bombing around the track in the feature race. Dad was weaving through the pack real good. The way he was driving, I thought we might get to carry another trophy home.

Mom and I squinted into the late afternoon sun; her cold hand squeezed mine whenever Number 6 even came close to kissing another stock car. I couldn't believe it was the last race of the year. I stared hard at the track, sopping up the race, storing it for the long winter ahead: the constant *tick-tick* of steel nicking steel; the swervy cars revving down the backstretch; smoldering rubber smelling as good as hot buttered popcorn.

And there was Dad, weaseling between two more cars down the homestretch—Mom's nails digging into my palms—gliding into turn one, and getting ready to slingshot out of turn two.

Then there was a spinout on the back straight that raised a curtain of dust. Number 6 went in...and didn't come out. All we heard was steel eating steel.

"Where's Daddy?" I asked Mom. *"Where's Daddy?"*

Looking as white as Ivory soap, she grabbed my hand and we ran toward the crash.

Took them a good hour to clear that pileup. Number 6 squirmed on the bottom of that steely stack, smushed and twisted and flattened.

Dad only bruised some ribs. But me and Mom took him to the hospital, anyway; Dick and Orrie hauled the Pontiac back to the house.

When we got home, Number 6 sat mangled in the dooryard, looking like some wicked knot in your shoelace that you couldn't untie in a million years. Dick and Orrie leaned quiet against the wreck.

Mom glanced at the car, looked at Dad like she was checking to make sure he really was in one piece, then went inside; tears nipped at her eyes.

I stared at the car, *my car*—the big red 6 crumpled and flaked— and started crying tears as thick and slow as dirty motor oil.

Dad pawed my head, put his arm around me, and we walked
out to the field; he smelled like burnt rubber. "We had a lot of
fun, didn't we, Andy?" he asked. "Didn't we, though?"

"Uh-huh," I said.

"That's all that matters. We had us one big ball."

My dad works real hard at Cheney's Mill. And still, some nights he doesn't come home till late, and his good-night kisses still smell like sawdust. But he doesn't sleep till noon on Saturdays anymore.

Most Saturdays you'll find me and Dad out in the pickup looking…hunting…keeping an eye out for another car…that certain old car…the one with just the right amount of dust clinging to the windshield.